CLOSING BELL

the Hunchback of Wall Street

by g.k. allen

Special thanks to the shadowy figures behind the scenes.

You know who you are…you are greatly appreciated!

"If ever I saw eyes that could see through me, and through tomorrow, they would be yours," Love Q.

This was the inscription on the framed picture on Fanny's nightstand, next to her bed. As Fanny slowly awoke, in her Park Avenue apartment, she gazed at her true loves graduation picture and said.

"Good luck on your first day, my love."

We take you back to the 1980's, the land of the free, home of the brave, in the big city, where shakers and movers are in full tilt. President Reagan "taking down the wall" in Germany. Madonna "vogueing" like a virgin. Bill Gates opening the proverbial flood gates of technology, in which he makes billions; Donald Trump creates and redefines New York City with Trump Towers. The city is bigger, brighter and shinier. Wall Street junk bonds hatch new millionaires.

Inside the great walls of the stock exchange on the Trade floor, people are standing still, waiting for the opening bell. All eyes are on the clock, waiting for the nine o'clock bell. As the second-hand sweeps down to the very last tick, the VIP's in the balcony are gathered for the ceremonial ringing of the opening bell. They are all poised and ready. Standing in the center of the VIP's is a young, boyishly handsome, college graduate named Quincy. He is the new V.P., and the honor of ringing the bell belongs to him. Standing next to him are several old-school, titans of Wall street. They conger up images of Mr. Monopoly; rich uncle, penny bags, top hat, waxed mustache and the formal wear, black tuxedo. Rico Wadsworth, the tallest of them all, and the number one guy, is the Uncle of Fanny. Fanny is betrothed to Quincy M. Otto, who is the new kid on the block.

Rico has his hand on Quincy's shoulder, as he is his protégé, and Rico says to Quincy.

"Go ahead my boy, this is your commanding moment! Make history!"

Quincy then hits the button and the opening bell rings. The trade floor goes crazy with motion. The stock exchange traders go into their routines; yelling, waving, and jumping around as they jockey for position. They buy, sell and trade everything, from pork bellies to commodities. Gold, silver, timber, navy beans, bonds, and the proverbial junk.

As the moment passes, the group around Rico shake hands with Quincy, congratulating him on his new position as the Acquisitions and Mergers V.P. As they move out of the main room and walk as a group down a hallway, Rico makes a speech:

"Well done son, now let's go retire to the Private V.I.P. room for cigars and brandy. We also have an omelet bar, no egg Mcduff for us, and we have a chef. Come on lad, you will get everything you deserve. Top of your class, captain of every sports team, now captain of this industry. You've served well in the pits. Now that you are marring my niece Fanny, you're right up there."

"Yes sir, up your Fanny!"

Quincy responds, "What"?

"I love Fanny of course, Tim up front and center!" Breaking through the cluster appears a greasy, slick haired, wrinkled, three-piece suit wearing, clip board, yes man.

"Quincy, may I have your signature on a few of these time sensitive document transfers ASAP"?

As they continue to talk and walk, Quincy looks perplexed and says,

"A few? You mean fifty!

There are over fifty pages!"

"Just every tenth one, the carbon paper copies it through to the others. Sign there in the x boxes. We have to hurry and get these into motion. We manage all the old money clients, large transactions."

"Are you sure about these x boxes?"

"That's for sure, I'd never play games when it comes to my x boxes!"

Quincy makes a concerned face but continues to sign them all. "Arr, X marks the spot!"

Rico replies, "yo, ho, ho, and a bottle of brandy." Tim chimes in, "Fifty pieces on a dead man's chest."

Rico winks at Tim.

"All I ask is for is a tall ship, the stars, and an omelet bar. Captains of industry, hoist the sails, load the cannons, scuttle the competition, by hook or by crook, dam the little man, full speed ahead!!!!!!"

Quincy is a little set back by what he is hearing, yet his focus is vigilant on his future with the love of his life.

Nothing else seems to matter when you are in the extreme passion filled bubble called love.

Later that afternoon, the surrounding areas of the big city showed signs of a fresh new spring like atmosphere. Trees and flowers blooming in the park, birds singing, hot dog carts frequent the streets, and horse drawn carriages clippety-clop, throughout. Street performers are abundant. Jugglers, mimes, and balloon peddlers holding every color balloon of the rainbow. 50 balloons frolicking in the breeze. The big cities finest on foot, walking a beat. Others on mounted steeds, equestrian protect and serve. Bicycles, tricycles, and unicycles, swerving around each other. Right in the midst of it all are Quincy and Fanny holding hands. He is dressed in a suit and she is a vision of loveliness, almost like a real live fairy Princess. Dressed in a beautiful summer dress, with a bright flower print. She almost blends in, with the beautiful bouquet of flowers Quincy pulls from behind his back to surprise her.

It was once said of hand holding, that it was one of the closest forms of intimacy. When we were very young, we hugged our teddy bears and our baby dolls, but we were in deeper need of affection. Emotion developed as we age, and hand holding showed a sign of maturity and commitment, as in grade school. Pairing off with someone you like, a public display of affection that was socially accepted. The Beatles even romanticized about it in their song, "I want to hold your hand". This still holds true for young lovers of then, who are now elderly. How sweet to walk down the street hand-in-hand, a woman and man. One another's heartbeat and pulse literally at your fingertips.

Fanny in her own humorous way, matching Quincy's sense of humor, takes the flowers, grabs some fruits and nuts in a bunch and places them on top of her head like a Carmen Miranda hat. "Coo Chi Coo Chi", as she lowers her summer dress to reveal naked shoulders. She rolls her shoulders and hips in a dancing motion like the original Chiquita banana girl. Without skipping a beat, Quincy produces a bush like handful of baby's-breath covering his lower face like a beard. While wearing sunglasses, and with a Scottish Brogue, he says,

"You can take the sheep from Scotland, but you can't take the scotch out of the sheep!"

Fanny replies, "That was Baaaaaad!"

Shortly thereafter the two are lounging on a large picnic blanket. Quincy now barefoot, lying on his back, and flying a red kite by a string tied to his big toe. He's wearing a large straw cowboy hat acquired at the open-air market, which shades his face as he pilots the red kite from his big toe. Fanny is laying against Quincy like a body pillow, propped up just enough to sip from her wine glass. She gazes at the red kite against the bright blue sky filled with scattered clouds, as she wistfully plays with the kite.

"So, this is how you fly a kite tied to your big toe after a large picnic lunch of fried chicken, apple pie and wine. I mean, what happens if a cop comes along and finds out that you been drinking you fail the breathalyzer test and he tickets you for a DUI. I mean really you want that to be on your permanent record drunk kite flying lazily with your big toe."

"My love if thou doth is displeased by my big toe, I shall tie it to something else and make it do you a figure 8. If it pleases thee!"

"Can thou make a slipknot that small?!"

"Small!" I'll give you small!" He rolls over onto her and continues rolling till the picnic blanket is like a big burrito. The kite keeps circling in the bright blue sky. They are rolled up like a burrito in their picnic blanket. Quincy starts to spout out.

"Bring, bring, bring…"

"What's that"?

Quincy replies in a Latin accent,

"It's the Tocco Bell, let me in it's cold outside, I have hot sauce!"

Fanny laughs uncontrollably as she is a part of this romantic public display of affection right in the middle of the park in broad daylight.

Later that evening, at Fanny's apartment, Fanny and Quincy are in bed watching television. They are side-by-side like an old married couple, snuggling, yet their feet protrude out from under the end of the blanket. They are playing footsies like kids at lunch break in elementary school. They display juvenile affection towards each other, which is to be expected as they are young lovers. They continue to flip channels until there is an old Jimmy Cagney, black and white movie playing on the television screen.

Apparently, in this old Jimmy Cagney movie, he yells,

"Top of the world Ma"!

Then he is gunned down by a hail of bullets and is killed. Quincy rolls over towards Fanny. He frequently imitates celebrities at a whim.

This time in a Jimmy Cagney voice,

"You dirty rodent"!

She replies, "That's rat! Q."

"Oh, you're a classy dame hey?"

She takes her hand and pushes it into the side of his face away from her and takes the channel changer from Quincy. She flips through the channels. Of all things, she finds Snow White and the Seven Dwarfs. Quincy starts to quip.

"Hi Ho, Hi Ho, Hi Ho," as he stares at Fanny.

"That's no way to greet a lady! You have lots of class Q. Yeah, unfortunately it's all low class ha, ha, ha, h,a."

"Right, seven little men with beards and one woman. Yeah that's really classy!"

"Hey, I like it, and Snow White melts grumpy with a kiss."

Well if that's all it takes, I got your bald headed little man with a beard, right here!"

Yeah, that's my Prince charming, the way you love me, here Prince, here Prince!" Again, Q without skipping a beat rolls over and gets on all four over Fanny as she tries to resist him.

"Wolf, Wolf, Wolf. Werewolf! Here, Wolf!"

Quincy reaches over and turns out the light on the nightstand. Out from the darkness Fanny laughingly says.

"Go away you dog, if we do it like this we will have puppies"! The two star struck lovers go at it until they are exhausted and falling asleep in each other's arms.

Love is wonderful, love is great. When two shall become one, then it's time to choose a cake.

Fanny and Quincy enter the front door of Nino's, a very upscale, fancy and expensive bakery. They are greeted by Nino himself. In some ways he reminds you of the Pillsbury dough boy, all dressed in white with a chef's hat tilted to one side.

"Welcome, my young friends, love is in the air, and my confections will convey your passion for all to share." He motions for them to follow him to a side room through some glass, French type, doors where there is a large amount of assorted baked goods. Nino leads them to a table and pulls out a chair for Fanny. Quincy sits next to her as Nino presents them with samples for their tasting delight.

Chocolate, Vanilla, Strawberry, and Marble, with the groom's red velvet cake in the shape of a football. Each sample is like a rainbow of textures, colors and flavors. Choosing the right cake is one of the first decisions they will make as a couple and sets the tone for the rest of their lives. Quincy seems to be tired and in need of some sleep. Franny nudges him.

"Seriously, can you stay awake, You? I know that you've been working late, but we have to decide what cake is ours."

"Yes, cake, good. Got it." Quincy's head bobs like he is going to nod off, which he does, face first, right into the red velvet grooms cake.

Fanny reacts, "Quincy, are you okay"!

He quickly responds as his head bobs back up face covered with frosting.

"Frosted Face They're Great"!

Nino stands back in surprise, not understanding the special love and sense of humor this couple shares. Quincy starts to sing.

"Sugar Pie Honey Bunch. I love you."

Fanny turns her head away and starts to lose it. She puts her head down in front of her covering her hands over her face as if ashamed. As she talks through prayer hands almost down to the tabletop.

"I can't believe you at times, just once, I wish..." Quincy leans forward, frosting and all to console her.

"But baby, Fanny sweetheart"?

Fanny replies, "But baby nothing". She in turn bobs back up from her side of the table. She has a face full of frosting as well. Nino rolls his eyes, as he witnesses the strange love birds firsthand. Fanny leans forward to kiss Quincy, but he stops her, grabs a tube of red frosting and applies it like lipstick. They kiss like two clowns in full makeup. Nino plays along.

"Has the happy couple come to a decision?"

Quincy replies, "Yes, I love the smell of lip balm in the morning"!

"Good choices, that face, I mean, cake, will serve funny, I mean plenty."

In the not too distant future, the overworked and underpaid groom to be, is fulfilling his new job obligations. The long hours and steadfast commitment to his job as a VP in charge of acquisitions and transactions seems to finally be paying off. Besides marrying the niece of his boss, he also has a private office, a personal secretary, 401(k) retirement plan matched by his employer, executive dining room privileges, as well as, a passkey to the company's fitness and spa center. Q is a young man climbing the corporate ladder to success.

As the day nears completion, he exits his office building through the underground parking area He flashes his employee badge to the young valet parking attendant. He nods and goes to retrieve Quincy's vehicle. Quincy looks at his watch several times while he waits for his vehicle. He is anxious to get by his loves side as it is the night of their rehearsal dinner and does not want to be late. A few moments pass, and the attendant pulls up to a seemingly impatient Quincy.

"There you go, sir. It's all gassed up, ready to go."

Quincy looks very confused. "That's not my car. You brought me the wrong car. I'm in a hurry."

"Sir, I beg your pardon, but I did match your employee ID badge to this vehicle. It's part of the young executive program and this is your company car!"

"Damn Sam I am green eggs and ham, stop the presses and hold the phone!"

Yes, sir, your car phone is in the console, press star for speakerphone and the speed dial is already set. Just press one for your significant other sir."

Quincy is grinning from ear to ear as he settles in the driver's seat of his, luxury vehicle, company car.

"This thing is loaded."

Like a kid with a new toy, he checks out all the options. He plays with the buttons. Electric seat adjustment, back and forth, back and forth, recline. He squirts the windshield with the wiper blade controller, which also has cruise control. The wiper blade switch back-and-forth, then come to stop. He adjusts his rear-view mirror and his door mirrors by push button. Quincy goes through a brief checklist like he's some kind of jet fighter pilot.

"I could get used to this."

He puts on his seat belt and puts the car in drive. Streets are buzzing at the end of the day, as people are in a hurry to go home and get out of the big city. Others, like, Quincy just need to get uptown, which is a short drive. Everything is bright and shiny like never before. Quincy has arrived and feels like a million bucks.

"Wait till Fanny, hell I don't have to wait I have a car phone! Hi, Ho, Hi, I can talk in my car as I go"!

The glow from the dashboard of Quincy's new company car illuminates his face.

"Fanny, can you hear me? Guess where I'm calling from? Hold on let me put this on speaker. Well, guess where I'm calling from?"

Fanny says, "Your new private office?"

"Wrong, no cigar. My little chickadee, I got a mobile phone, in my shiny new company car, perks of my job, just for being the new VP."

"Mr. Big."

"Yes ma'am, an office on wheels. I'm running a little late."

Fanny replies, "Is that safe to talk on a car phone while you're driving?"

Q says, "It's on speaker sweet cheeks, no worry, can't wait to get out of this traffic and open this thing up."

"Q, I have to ask you, will you still love me when I'm old and gray?"

He replies, "Grandma Walton always looked hot!"

"What about you, when I'm bald, wrinkled and fat sitting in a creaking rocking chair and then you realize the creaking is coming for me?"

"As long as you still rock."

"Okay, so how do you feel about sex at 60?"

"Ummm?"

"Or is that too fast? Because I can put this thing in cruise control at 55, and the seats recline, and there's even a tilt steering wheel for more headroom."

"Don't threaten me with a good time. Cruisin' in the new ride, maybe?"

Meanwhile, the city traffic seems to become more congested, as Quincy tries to beat all the traffic signals as he maneuvers like a Daytona 500 contestant. The steel and concrete jungle that surrounds him seems to be closing in on him. Blocking out the sunlight as well as the signal to his mobile car phone.

"You still there Fanny?"

Her reply is a broken up, every other word, slowly fading.

"I, you, me, soon."

"Sorry, I'm going through a dead zone, I said dead zone, talk later. Love you!"

Then the phone resonates, "You have been disconnected. If you feel like you've been disconnected in error, please hang up and dial again."

"I hate being disconnected! But I'm going to make that red light."

He speeds up, then realizes the light is going to turn red and he quickly applies the brakes. Quincy realizes he has no breaks something has malfunctioned.

"OH SHIT!" Sudden impact was inevitable. There was no escaping the fact, no two things can occupy the same space. One being a heavy-duty garbage truck, the other Quincy's company car, and a third contender, a city bus. Like no other sound you could ever imagine, smashing, crashing, steel scraping, banging, tires screeching, a mangled accordion mass of combined destruction. Then a complete moment of silence. A cease-fire of inertia and brute force. Smoke and dust begin to settle on this hell beast mangled creation. 0% survival, 100% devastation!

The intersection looks like a war zone gone bad. Emergency vehicles and first responders are now in route as you can hear their sirens. The vehicles are caught in the gridlock. A crowd on the sidewalk accumulates, as the bystanders that have witnessed this horrific collision stare blankly in disbelief. The fire department, the police department, the paramedics all go into action upon reaching the site. The garbage truck driver and bus driver were unharmed, as they tell police what happened. Emergency crews swarm to the automobile in the middle of the mess. A paramedic got in close, reaching through the drivers broken window.

"I got a pulse and he's still breathing"!

The firemen bring out the Jaws of Life. In a blink of an eye, they peel back the driver's door from the mangled mess. As the paramedics come in, they carefully extract the driver of the automobile with one swift movement. They place him on a padded gurney and pack him up snug like a mummy, to contain his life fluids. Only time and expediency, could rectify the situation. Police on horseback proceed to clear the sidewalks and make a path, like Moses parting the Red Sea. A slim chance in a race against time and the Grim Reaper. The world keeps spinning as the inner-city hospital is dimly lit and at capacity as another day dawns. Quincy is in an old-fashioned hospital bed. Packed with bandages from head to toe and is on life support. Only his right eye is uncovered as he fades in and out of consciousness. His future is very bleak.

Fanny is there by his side, still wearing her bride-to-be, rehearsal dinner, dress.

"If you can hear me, I'm right here by your side, don't try to speak, they have you on support to help you. Rest, heal, and let the meds do their job. You have the best taking care of you. Just do whatever they say, I love you!"

She continues her vigilance next to his bed in the makeshift ICU room on the first floor. Her makeup is smeared from crying and sleeping next to him in a big chair. Hopeful wishes, from one soul mate to another. Eventually she goes home and leaves him in the care of the hospital staff. She must surrender to the stress and the disbelief of this tragic reality.

Days later, a priest is in the chair next to Quincy's bedside, giving him last rights.

"Pox de cum".

Quincy seems to react ever so slightly as he is trapped in a motionless nightmare of a ravaged body and soul. The passage of time is slow upon floating in and out of consciousness. Not knowing whether or not you are you and to what capacity do you exist. Several weeks have passed at this point in time. It's in the middle of a shift change, as a young fresh-faced nurse comes in to his room, to check his stats.

"You gave us a scare, glad you are still with us. You are off the breathing machine! You still have oxygen attached to your nasal intake, I'm going to increase your drip level, and you just relax. Keep up the breathing, you are doing great!"

Hospital staff start to flow into Quincy's room; people in white coats with stethoscopes, and a few doctors gather beginning to banter back and forth verbally.

"He's responding well to the mega steroids treatment. He is strong-willed."

"He'll need that when the reconstructive surgery begins. Thank goodness the John Hopkins team will be here to do the rebuild."

"Doctors have you seen the x-rays. It's like a mosaic puzzle of bones on his entire right side."

"He's functioning as normal as possible, for having been crushed and rearranged. Yet, his vitals are significantly amazing!"

"If they don't start reconstruction soon, he'll pull a Joseph Merrick!"

One of the younger doctors whisper under his breath. "Elephant man?"

"Left untreated, it will heal abnormal and disfigured."

Although his thought processes are fogged by medication and is unable to speak, Quincy hears the doctors clearly. He reacts in the confines of his own thoughts.

"Crushed, orange crush I love that soda. Who's this Abby normal, Dumbo was an elephant. Baby, baby of mine, rest your head close to my heart, never to part, baby. Baby I need your lovin, got's to have, sugar pie Honey Bunch. My panties are definitely in a bunch. I've got a lovely bunch of coconuts, goodness gracious great balls of fire. Uncontrollable mind babbling, somebody stop me. Oh, wow, warm fuzzy feeling, the morphine drip....

Top of the World Ma!"

Feeling no pain, Quincy has some peace and quiet. Only to be disturbed by the voice of Rico Wadsworth.

"I don't know if you can comprehend, but all your medical has been taking care of. Don't worry about work you've done more than most men in one lifetime. My niece is devastated by all of this. If she ever hears tales of all those inside trades and junk-bond scams, well it's between you and me. You've served the company well, all the files indicating you, have been secured."

The expression on Rico's face is like that of a crazed mad scientist. Standing over Quincy, he lets out a short burst of an evil genius type laugh. Just the two of them in the dimly lit hospital room. The lights flicker, and Rico Wadsworth disappears.

Back in the big city hospital, sometime later. Quincy is still wrapped up like a mummy with one eye open. There is a Doctor and a strange man in a shirt, tie and jacket.

"This is Special Agent Hogart, and he wants to ask you a few questions. I told him we are limited to a "Yes" or "No" reply. One finger is for yes and two fingers are no."

"You may leave us now Doctor."

"Yes or No, Quincy did you realize that your brakes on your company vehicle were tampered with?"

Quincy puts up two fingers.

"No"...., you can see, somebody was making an attempt on your life. Is there someone you trust with your life and trade secrets that might want you dead?"

Quincy's fingers are shaking as he puts up two fingers.

"That's a "No" as well. It's clear that your accident was no accident"! Take care Quincy, we'll be in touch.

Quincy is awoken later in the day by doctors talking and making chatter about his condition. Most of these doctors will assist in his reconstructive surgery. The moment of truth has come. The doctors remove the bandages from Quincy's head. Doctors are standing at the foot of Quincy's bed waiting. The eldest doctor in the group begins to speak.

"As you can see he's very disfigured. His injuries have begun to heal. One eye is considerably lower than the other, and the jaw line is dislocated. Along with a curved spinal injury to the back. Where do we begin?"

A young doctor pipes up.

"So, facial reconstruction, if he is to have a chance at normalcy?"

The eldest doctor pipes up again.

"The experimental steroid growth hormones will resonate 20 years! Everyone please step outside in the hallway. We need to have a little space and some privacy. Someone dim the lights and please maintain silence. Quincy, you have been through a lot. When you look into the mirror, look at your right side first, as it will be the more normal side. Then slowly, you may take a look at the rest of your face. Remind yourself you've been through a lot of pain and anguish. It's going to be apparent in your looks. Mirror, please."

The youngest doctor hands the eldest doctor the mirror, in turn, he slowly hands it over to Quincy.

"I know reality feels like it's all a bad dream young man, but we all care about you and we are here to help you.

Quincy, for the first time in a long time, can now put a face to his pain and suffering from his tragic accident. With his face turned sideways, Quincy slowly peeks into the mirror. As he turns the mirror he sees the ugliness and the destruction. He breaks down and cries out loud,

"No, no, no, no, why God why!"

His high pitch wines sound like a coyote in the wilderness after a kill! Feeling hurt and all alone, Quincy spins out of control! He throws the mirror out into the hallway, and the mirror shatters. Nurses scramble into his room. The lights are flipped on. He continues to throw his bedpan, channel changer, and whatever else he can get his hands on. The elder doctor yells,

"Nurse sedate him now!"

"No, no, no…." Quincy succumbs to the injection. He runs out of energy falls back onto his pillow. His face wincing in pain, although it's hard to tell on the disfigured side.

Meanwhile, uptown, in a Park Avenue apartment, Fanny is on the phone.

"I don't understand why I can't see him, I know he's disfigured, he needs me…

Okay, call me if things change, thank you, good night, ohh… before you hang up!"

It's too late, the hospital hung up on her, she completes her thoughts out loud. "Tell him I love him!"

She drops the phone onto the floor. She can hear the disconnecting dial tone. Fanny rolls over on her loveseat, where she was sitting, hugs a silk embroidered pillow, and cries herself to sleep. Per chance to dream, to forget, and hope that this tragic reality is all but a bad nightmare.

Still, on the other side of town, in a dimly lit hospital, there is a skeleton crew working the night shift. Taking care of a disheveled young man, the night nurse checks on Quincy. She touches his shoulder and pulls up his blankets to keep him as comfortable as possible. On her way out of the room she is greeted by the same priest that once gave Quincy his last rights. He sneaks past to sit by Quincy's side. The priest leans over and puts a chain with a cross on it around Quincy's neck. He silently says a few prayers, then speaks to Quincy in a low tone. Quincy is wrapped in fresh bandages with only one eye clearly present. The priest is a wearing a hooded robe. He speaks with a slight accent.

"I know your times have been troubled a world of despair. Yet you don't want to go underground until you have to, and when you do, you will hold your head high. The Lord has a plan for you. You survived these past eight months for a reason. I myself am here on missionary work. I help the unwanted, I work out of the basement of the cathedral, one day at a time. We pray, we live, we exist, and sometimes all we have is the struggle. Just ask Monsignor Dominic. He barely keeps the cathedral functioning, but he brings hope! Yes, my friend, you are Charlie Brown's sad little Christmas tree! My mission is here for now. Soon you will be strong enough to get out of that bed. I will keep a vigilance with you tonight as you sleep."

As the priest goes to the bathroom, he hangs his hooded robe on the back of the bathroom door. When finished, he goes back and sits in the chair in the dark corner of the room by Quincy's bedside, near the window. The dividing curtain is drawn around Quincy's bed as he sleeps. All is quiet until Quincy is startled. He wakes up, suddenly sitting up in his bed. Attached to an IV on a pole with wheels, he attempts to stand up using the IV unit. His face and body are still wrapped in bandages. He struggles as his crooked body staggers alongside the bed very slowly. He's heading towards the bathroom. A night light is on in the bathroom. He pulls the cord for the nurse, but there's no response. Just outside the hospital room, lays a nurse knocked out on the floor. A shadowy figure with a flashlight is standing over her. A man in a security guard uniform enters into Quincy's room. The security guard stands quietly just on the outside of the curtain that is drawn near Quincy's bed. Quincy's vocal sounds are a little exaggerated when he tries to talk. Similar to that of a stroke survivor, talking out of the side of their mouth. Strangely, what he hears, makes himself laugh just a little bit. He sounds like Elmer FUD.

"Here I sit all brokenhearted, dropping a deuce! Houston, we have splashdown, that's cold water, pretty drippy Yuk, that trains been backed up for eight weeks. Nurse! I finished dropping a deuce!"

Still, there is no reply, as he pulls the cord. He hears a noise and peeks out through the crack of the bathroom door. With his one good eye, Quincy sees the man in the security uniform, just on the outside of the drawn curtain. He's fumbling with the oxygen knobs on the wall. He squirts some kind of lighter fluid on Quincy's divider curtain.

"Quincy, you dumb ass, you should have died the first time! Look what you made me do!"

Quincy is scared as he realizes what's going on, whispering to himself, "They tried to kill me!"

The security guards shadowy figure backs away. Then, through the hospital door Quincy sees a lit cigarette being tossed by a hand wearing a gold Rolex. The lighter fluid-soaked curtain ignites and starts to burn. Quincy, thinking as quickly as possible, grabs the heavy hooded robe off the bathroom door. He falls into the wet running shower stall, closing the bathroom door behind him. Then it happens. Kaboom!! A loud explosion. Balls of fire blast the priest and the windows out of the side of the building, leaving, no trace of the priest's existence. Left behind is a walk-out opening on the ground floor, trimmed with flames. The hell beast of destruction struck for a second time. This time, leaving one dead… cremated actually! Slowly, Quincy, in the hooded robe, emerges from the bathroom, grasping his IV pole on wheels. Slinking along, holding on tight to keep up right. He goes through the glowing fiery arches of the now wide-open ground zero, hospital room. As fire alarms and sirens go off, he starts to hobble down the sidewalk into the darkness of night. He's feeling half crazy, almost crying, mumbling to himself…

"This outpatient program sucks, no pretty release nurses on staff, nothing, I had to release myself into my own hands, everyone deserves a good release. Damn, I forgot to wipe, when you're walking down the street, something, warm at your feet, diarrhea! Just shut up and walk Quincy, or they will kill you! That's twice, third time's a charm, there after my lucky charms, magically delicious, my ass! I'll hide, like a stray cat, me out meow me ouch, it hurts, oh the pain. Oh, the suffering, gloom, despair and agony on me. If it weren't for bad luck, I'd have no luck at all. Shut up Quincy just keep moving. Left, right, left, right, oh my Lord, my nuts are tight."

Quincy is moving down the sidewalk into the dark alleys of the big city. He continues limping down the dirty city streets and heads for the nearest subway station. Just before he reaches the subway station entrance, an old scary woman jumps out of the dark alleyway stopping Quincy dead in his tracks. She is very old and looks homeless wearing multi-layers of odd clothing.

"Where you goin' padre? Why not use the express?!"

Quincy, staring out from under his robe replies. "Express?"

"Yes!" As her voice cracks, she hits the handle on the side of the building and the sidewalk elevator opens up. Apparently, it's an old stock handler's passage to the underground for storage. The old lady grabs the IV stand on wheels and pulls it away from Quincy. At first she seems like she is trying to help him, but then rips it away. The IV still attached to his arm is disconnected. He quickly grabs the elevator rail as it starts to go down. She stands up on the sidewalk watching him descend.

"Expressed to where?" Quincy is at a loss.

She cackles like an old witch, "Hell you freak!" The sidewalk elevator closes flat over Quincy's head as he disappears into the unknown.

The next morning Fanny, residing in her Park Avenue apartment, is watching the television news. There is a reporter on the television screen with a sub caption "Breaking News". This particular reporter is standing just outside the hospital where the authorities have it guarded. There is a large gaping hole on the first floor of the ICU.

"This just in: apparently there was an accidental explosion of an oxygen line break that has left one dead and a night nurse injured. Details at 11."

While watching the newscast, she gets on the phone and calls her uncle, Rico Wadsworth.

"I just saw the news report, Uncle are you sure it was Quincy?"

"Yes, I'm sorry to say but the best man in my security division has confirmed it!"

"But, but he was getting better…"

She loses it, and cries profusely.

"Fanny, I know this is not much comfort, but, he's in a better place now, he suffered tremendously. We must start looking to the future. You were briefed recently about the inconsistencies that surrounded the dearly departed. There was going to be an inquiry as to the insider trading and the millions of lost profits by the trades commission. His name will never be tarnished with an investigation. Lord only knows where all those millions went."

Fanny still crying, "I don't believe it, I don't believe any of it!"

Somewhere in a dark undisclosed location, there is a candle flickering. Quincy is still wrapped up in bandages, lying on a bed. His surroundings are unfamiliar, a small bedroom with antique furniture, stone walls and no window. As the creaky, old wooden door to the bedroom opens slowly, in walks a holy man, also in a hooded robe. Monsignor Dominic approaches Quincy with a tray of food that consists of bread and soup. Placing it next to the flickering candle at the bedside on a small table, he says,

"Are you awake padre?"

Quincy responds, "Yes."

"If you are able, we have something to eat. You need your strength to heal after the explosion. Quincy an angel must have been watching over you to bring you safely back to this cathedral. I know who you are, and I have your name tag from the hospital. Somehow you have the robe of the church from Padre Paul? He must have been keeping vigilance over you the time of the hospital explosion."

The Monsignor blesses Quincy with the sign of the cross. "Pox de cume father Paul,"

Quincy mumbles in response,

"Pox de cume Dominic, nobis to tu to tum."

"We are also educated, my son."

"I think, it hurts to think!"

"Take it easy as you are in trusting hands, your physical recovery will be long, lots of time for your mental strength. We can leave the bandages on till you are ready. We must keep things clean and change them often. I had already done so when I brought you in. I know you have a lot of questions, all in due time. The good Lord bless you and keep you under his care, now eat and rest my son."

Much time has passed since then. Michael Jackson is deceased, banks have failed, many foreclosures, many homeless. AIG and the war in the sands continue. Stimulus packages, Jay Leno retired from the Tonight Show, Conan, his replacement fails, and Jay Leno comes back from retirement. The president not only gets a new dog, he also instills a government bailout of the auto companies. Unemployment looms. There may be electric cars in the future. Everybody wants to go green. Yet some things never change. The big city is overflowing as the creatures of the night, live under the cloak of darkness. The socially unacceptable, the homeless, the unwanted. Many of them are families, many veterans, old and new, some are crazy, but they are definitely not stupid because survival of the streets demands it!

In the darkness, traveling the back streets and alley ways, is a large pushcart the size of a delivery van. It's slowly making its way, being pushed by one individual, stopping at back doors and dumpsters. This sinister creature of the night pushing the large oversize cart, is collecting recyclables bottles, cans, etc. Not an ordinary person, but one born out of necessity. Still wearing the robe, Quincy is pushing the large cart effortlessly. He has developed large muscles and strength, like that of a world-class bodybuilder, yet not so upright, and favoring one side as to the other. He is Hercules unchained. He had no choice but to go to extreme strength as it was his will. It is the survival of the fittest. His arms and legs are cloaked as his curved hunched over back inhibits his ability to stand straight. Even his hands are muscular, from years of hard manual labor collecting and pushing the street cart. Uptown suits wish they had his fortitude of which came of necessity, as they immolate strength in their Pilates and spin classes.

Quincy continues down a dark area of the street until he reaches a dim lit area of the city. His cart is overflowing with recyclables. There is a guard at a gate next to a sign that reads, recycle, USA cash for recyclables. Quincy approaches the guard.

"Another abundant load, sir?"

"The holidays are coming, more needs for the homeless."

" You must have some crazy ass muscles after pushing that oversize cart for the past 20 years, hold on a sec..."

The guard brings out a bag full of cans.

"Here's my weeks' worth of cans."

The guard tosses the bag on top of Quincy's pushcart.

"Bless you, my son."

"Go ahead. The lines are short tonight."

Quincy pushes the large cart forward. There is a line of about 20 people, all shapes and sizes. Mostly street people with shopping carts, handcarts, and some with large garbage bags. The line in the recycle yard gets shorter. Quincy and his oversize pushcart are next. The tally man makes an accounting,

"Onto the scales, please."

Quincy pushes the cart forward, the tally man checks the readout.

"Wow, talk about your dangerous catch! You broke your own record this time! You on the juice? That cart is loaded!"

"Yup. Jesus juice, purely salvation powered!"

"Amen to that. Happy holidays. Here's your cash, keep that envelope in a safe place, Padre. Thanks, tally man, tally me bananas, daylight, and I want to go home, Day Oh Day Oh!"

Quincy continues, slowly pushing his large cart out of the gate and into the darkness.

Unbeknownst to Quincy, there is a small group of three street thugs gathered on the next corner. They soon intersect under a dim streetlight. All of the thugs are dressed in leather jackets, they stand in front of the pushcart, and make it stop.

"That's far enough freak hand over the cash!"

There is no answer and the thugs rush to the backside of the cart. There is no Quincy. They panic and rush around the 6-foot-high cart.

"Where's the freak. He's got the cash!"

From the top of the cart corner Quincy stands as tall as possible, larger-than-life, and starts to pitch glass bottles like a major league pitcher. 90 miles an hour, hitting the thugs upside their heads as they duck and run for cover.

"Catfish Hunter, Nolan Ryan, Cy Young, Mark "The Bird" Fidrych, eat your hearts out!"

Still pitching bottles at the runaway thugs.

"Willie Hernandez, no maas, no aqui, balance the ball, but I like your sister speedy, let's go home!"

Quincy makes it safely below the surface of the streets. Quincy, the shadowy figure comes up the tunnel. He steps into the light and looks around. He sees the people of the underground, homeless, unwanted, and hungry. Helpless of all ages, shapes, sizes, genders and color. He stops in the camp of a temporary dwelling, stands as tall as possible, clears his throat, and lights up a Coleman lantern.

"Hello, I'm a giver not a taker, a friend, not a foe, ain't the pimp looking for no hoes. I ain't the man trying to learn you into a program!"

People are battered looking at him. They look up and start to believe him as he opens up a big duffel bag. One homeless man responds,

"Leave me alone, I don't need you, I don't need anyone, I don't need anything!"

"Let me guess, in your suitcase, you have an ashtray, paddle game, remote control, some matches, the lamp, a magazine, and that chair you are sitting on."

"Who are you, how did you know??"

"I'm just like you down and out, shunned by society misunderstood wrongly labeled. I got lost and found innocence. In, or, out of my mind, a fashion statement for plight, life knocks me down, but before it counts to 10, I get up the next day to fight!"

A woman in the back speaks up.

"Save it. Mohammed Ali, what are you selling?"

"I'm giving you, not selling, I'm just asking that you just listen to what I'm telling!"

A homeless youth spouts off.

"Oh, here it comes, amen, hallelujah, whatever, can you pull my mom and dad out of your magic bag? They left me down here to get high. I'm all alone."

"I'm sure they will be right back."

"Yeah, you're right, they have only been gone from here three years now!"

Quincy literally jumps back. It gets everybody's attention.

"Ouch, I'm sorry, no I can't do that, but I can give you hope. I know most of you beg, borrow, and steal. I know how you feel, you didn't get a fair deal. You need a square meal. A safe place to sleep, some things to keep, a little charity, faith and hope, and I don't mean the ones at the scores VIP room! But back to Howard Stern. If you beg and people back you up, bathe before you beg. I give you hope! On a rope, so soap!"

He holds up a soap on a rope like the shape of a bell. It smells like fresh pine.

"Everybody gets one, step up, wash away your blues, wash, clean your act up, don't make the body odor a sneak attack. Relax, forget your troubles make some bubbles. If cleanliness is next to godliness. Don't smell like the bowels of hell, you may be mortified. You got to get fortified. With homemade lye, no die. No toxic stuff that can make you off. You may not be pretty, but you ain't got to be dirty!"

Then a short homeless man replies,

"You talk crazy doesn't he, ha, ha, ha, ha, ha!"

"Takes one to know one, you get two hopes of soap on a rope. One for your invisible friend, help him to help yourself. Wash all 2000 parts!"

Another homeless guy in the back steps forward.

"Can I wash myself as fast as I want to?"

"It's up to you, just use the soap and maybe you can change the world's perspective one stinky ass at a time. Is it me or is it a cotton and ass convention tonight? Hi, my name is Bob and I'm a recovering stinker. My stink was so strong, Fear Factor wanted me for one of their fears. The EPA wanted me to file a report whenever I broke wind. Paris wanted to bottle my fragrance and sell it to the French as a roll-on. My feet swelled up in my shoes because my odor eaters were bloated. One time I rode the subway and played pull my finger with Sponge Bob crusty pants and 28 passengers were taken away by ambulance for affixation. People passed out on the spot, a hazmat team came out and scrubbed down crusty pants and me, but look at Bob today! Bob step forward."

Pushing his way through the crowd of homeless people suddenly appears Bob, a slender man. He has on a Saturday Night Fever, John Travolta type suit. Although some of his white ensemble has various stains in different places; armpits and seams, he spins like he is on a catwalk.

"Thanks, Bob. The new spring line from Goodwill. I think that was Ben Affleck suit from Gigli. Yet, Bob backslides sometimes and when he does he just shakes it down his leg and gets on with his life. You crazy deuce on the run champions, take it to the alley and commit to a drop-in throw. It's about communication. What were you wanting to convey? I know some of you homeless belong in a home, but those are places are all stacked up like crazy in the winter. That's when the underground resort starts to fill up. That's why I am down here seven times a week, two shows a day and a matinee and Sundays. Don't be a dope, use the soap!"

The crowd reacts by mingling with one another. They all get in line in and crowd around Quincy as they hold their hands out to receive their hope, the soap on a rope.

The flip side of all the skyscrapers and concrete above ground is as amazing as the underbelly. They are the roots of the city. Most of the underground tunnels are part of the subway system. The light from the manhole covers in the street vents shine like spotlights on the walls and the tunnels of the abandoned subway entrances. Down a long way, there is a man with one bucket of paint; brushes and a large duffel bag. This particular man is a graffiti artist. It's his way of giving hope to the homeless. To those that tread the underground lifestyle. There is a wall glowing in the light, a larger graffiti is being completed. One of the corners of the work is a deformed Picasso looking man in the bell tower of the cathedral, pulling the ropes, ringing the bells. As the man continues to paint, the shadowy figure comes up behind him. The artist without pause, feels somebody approaching.

"Hello Padre."

"You heard me coming? I'm at a loss Van Go, like your bad ear."

Quincy stands next to the artist as they look at the new wall of art.

"No, I smelled you coming!"

"Smelled? I bathed!"

"Yeah, ode to Pine, thy soap on a rope shaped like a bell."

"It sells during the holidays."

"Yeah, we are all starving artist at this point, and how many times do I have to tell you to stop calling me Van Go, I know I have one bad ear, but that's because I got drunk with the rats! Unfortunately, they were not whispering sweet little nothings into that ear!"

"Hey, this painting looks good, the freedom to live unobserved, the freedom to create artwork!"

"This place is freedom from rent, a refuge if you will."

"I have a simple request, …the bell ringer in the tower?"

"Is it too descriptive?"

"Just a little!"

There is a likeness of Quincy, lit up by the manhole, sunlight coming through. It shows all of Quincy's deformities.

"That was over 20 years ago when I painted that corner, I only painted what I saw! Like a cave painting of Neanderthals."

"What no mastodons, no sabretooth tigers?"

"Watch this, Padre"

Van Go takes a brush and splatters like a machine gun across the corridor. Painting with accuracy, he blots out the face of the bell ringer.

"Now that's art!"

"You have an eye for art."

Quincy shakes his head. "Thanks? No depth perception, but the colors must work for you. There are a lot of one appendage people out there. Lance Armstrong, tour de France, one dangler in his pants!"

"That is so true, if you would like to pose for a portrait, we could go down aways and do some justice to that mug of yours."

"Thanks, but no thanks, keep up the good work though."

Quincy turns and starts to walk away from the artist

"Hey you can't just walk away from me."

Quincy turns and tosses some rope with some soap to the artist and he catches it.

"Thanks. Smell you later!"

"Hey, don't forget the Halloween party at the uptown pavilion, I hand forged 40 tickets, a real work of art!"

"Great, the gang will love the Gray Poupon and the surf and turf buffet. The Lone Pine Entourage roles again!"

Late at night in the fancy inner-city restaurant that never sleeps... A young waiter is cleaning a table. There sits a lot of uneaten food on the plates, lobster, stakes, roles, and salads all untouched. He brings a big tray, cleans it all away then goes to the back-alley door. There in the alley, is a large book bag next to his coat. He looks around the then scrapes off food into a bag and puts it in the big oversized book bag, while covering it with his coat. Todd the waiter, is behind on rent, gas, and electric again. He will never go hungry because of his part-time job, ala, table scraps. All his duties are nearly complete inside the restaurant, and he is soon on his way. He leaves out the back door, grabs his bag, his coat, and he goes down the back alleyway into the dark, until he reaches a certain fire escape balcony. A young woman is waiting with a blanket around herself just one flight up. Shivering, as she tries to keep warm. She smiles as she notices Todd down in the alley with his book bag. He comes closer and Sally looks down upon him.

"Romeo, Romeo, what fourth yon bag of ravenous delights do you bring upon my moonlit balcony. Come closer, sir."

Just then as he starts to climb the ladder he's pulled back by a thug and his street friends. The biggest thug starts to manhandle Todd.

"Romeo, you fag's actor gimme that!

He takes the book bag, he tries to stand up to the other thug holding him as they try to beat him up. Suddenly a large pushcart is barreling down upon the thugs and the big thug yells,

"Look out Chino!"

They all jump to the side as a cart crashes and hits a wall. They start to get back up and a shadowy figure jumps on them, then takes the book bag and beats them with it until they submit and runaway. Quincy, the shadowy wild figure says,

"I believe this is yours."

He hands the bag back to Todd.

"Thanks, wild and strange man. Who are you, kind sir? As you are this ladies champion."

"It's, no never mind, just follow me and I will show you to a temporary haven".

They gladly follow Quincy down the sidewalk and get to the elevator that Quincy knows all too well. They step on it and disappear as the elevator top closes behind them. Now they are down under the streets. There are more lights than the first time he was there. Lots of used, twinkle, Christmas lights. Groups of people huddling in different corners. Some have really old televisions and furniture.

Bunk beds with younger families, all off the wet floors on forklift crates. Whatever they found above ground that might be salvaged. All useful to the homeless. The three of them walk through the small village of homeless then look at each other. Sally looks amazed.

"How? Why?"

"Well, as you must know when the homeless shelters are full of or the friends that lets you sleep on their couch and they lose their job and home because they are only one paycheck ahead of being homeless. There are 108,000 homeless in places like the Big Apple."

Todd the waiter quips, "Lots of wormholes in the Apple!"

"It's rough, enough being a woman, but there's children!"

"The lucky ones are still with their mom and dads. When they get to the shelter, it's a first-come, first-served. If you have bad timing, 'cause you just got mugged and someone stole your watch and you wake up in an alley. You're lucky to be alive. The street thugs prey on the weak. What you got, they want, you don't even want to know the death rate amongst the homeless! I can't get to most of them before it's too late."

"Todd and I were okay living above the dance studio. Until the street thugs broke in, while Todd was working. I got knocked down and broke my foot. I lost my apartment and my job. It's like the thugs knew what to do. The Wadsworth Corporation, took over my building."

Quincy mumbles and growls to himself.

"Mr. Wadsworth, Wall Street giant, he's picking on the little people, wasn't that enough that he scammed all my clients and buried me, and now this!"

Todd inquires, "You said what about your clients?" "I said he was shamelessly defiant What's next, extermination of the weak!"

Sally acts confused. "What?"

Quincy starts moving around nervously.

"What do I know, I'm just an underground circus freak, hey, watch this!"

He juggles three bars of his soap on the rope in the air. Todd is amazed

"That will get you a cup of coffee and maybe a bowl of soup, lone stranger!"

Quincy precedes to lead the young couple to a dry safe spot amongst all the rest and they settle in for the night.

The next day there is a commotion at the subway platform. A crowd is gathered around. As the crowd subsides, there is Quincy. He is draped over a person laying on the tracks. It's Bob!

"Bob, you're my number one guy. What happened?" Bob is laboring to talk as he is in a lot of pain.

"The last thing I remember is, I was waiting for the last train, some thugs crowded me and I fell onto the tracks. I bounced off the windshield of the train and hit the wall. I looked up and there were 3 thugs, not street like, but military dressed in black! They were yelling, you squatters get out!"

"Security goons Bob?"

"They had patches on their sleeves. A big W with a thunderbolt through it."

"Wadsworth! Bob stay calm the paramedics are on their way, Bob, if you hurt just smell your armpits! You are a reck Bob, where's the soap I gave you?"

Bob laughs and cries and coughs. At the same time.

"I just got a job at the falafel cart padre, the owner reeks too, I just wanted to blend in, Q!"

"What you mean, Q?"

"I Googled you a long time ago, I know who you are, I know a lot of things, I just have a problem staying straight! When you first came into the area and became my friend, there was a look in your eye, your good eye. I saw your, compassion, and betrayal. Now I know where the betrayal is, maybe a touch of loss, and lost love!"

Bob looks away as if he is shaken emotionally.

"Just shut up Bob, save your energy till the medics get here!"

Quincy motions to one of their other friends. The lady comes and takes over for Quincy holding Bob till the medics come, Quincy then turns and disappears.

Shortly thereafter, down at the other subway tunnel, the subway train whizzes by, and as it passes, there's a shadowy figure on the back of the train's roof. It comes to a stop at a platform and there are three security thugs rustling groups of homeless sleeping on a bench. They began to manhandle and push around the homeless between themselves, the tallest of the goon's yells.

"When are you people going to learn, stay out of the underground hideouts or you will all be exterminated like rats! It's not going to be safe when the pest-control gases hit the tunnels! You don't want to be around! Trust me, go ask Rusty Bob, he will tell you!"

One of the older people gets pushed down, while the other goon pokes him with a nightstick.

"Get the point old man!"

Then, from out of nowhere, there is a noise from the top of the exit stairs, like rolling thunder only scarier and louder. The shortest thug runs over to the stairs and gets rolled over by a big metal snack machine that flies down the stairs. A bowling ball knocking down 10 pins, a perfect strike. Another goon runs over to help him and gets bashed from behind by a large trashcan over his head, knocked out and then rolled over on his side. The lights flicker in the subway like a strobe light. The last goon is swept off his feet by a Cowboy's rope, like a fat calf, rodeo roped in the flickering light. Dragged by his heels, like a rag doll, he is whisked away by the tightening rope up, the exit stairs and out of sight. Topside of the dark city streets, with a rope tied to his ankles, he is dragged through the wet gutters of the street. Tied to the back of a street sweeping truck, kicking and screaming until it drives out of sight.

The following day. A large ray of light shines through the street drains on the graffiti inside one of the tunnels. There are paintings on the wall. You can see many faces painted, old and new. The artist is painting a new face, it's crusty Bob's! The artist is putting the finishing touches on the likeness. Then Quincy shows up behind the painter.

"When?"

"Shortly after you left, I showed up and led the medics to him. He passed away in the night while he was sleeping."

"Rest in peace, Bob! He was a good egg, even though he smelt like a bad one, boiled left out in the sun under a pile of sweat socks that were left out from the 1950s Globetrotters locker room! A fitting tribute to the dearly departed!"

"Yeah, life stinks!"

"There's a lot of faces up there, Van Go! The forgotten, unwanted, homeless. Lots of vets, as well as this guy, was a bronze star winner and in Vietnam. This guy was once the mayor of New York. Lots of other politicians, is that Bob Denver, Gilligan, poor little buddy. They did call him. Sailor! He went from a tropical island to a subterranean River, I think Ginger and Mary Ann are still around. I could use a coconut cream pie, although sometimes Ginger creamed my anatomy."

"Talking about cream, the news reported an attack about three security guards in the subway. One crushed by a snack machine, the other got trashed and, and the last was dragged five blocks until the street sweeping guy stopped, to have a coffee."

"See the subways aren't safe for anybody."

"Five blocks, good thing he didn't get on the expressway."

"So, what if he did, he could have used the carpool lane."

"I think you have to have the extra person inside the moving vehicle."

"In the bus, on the bus, under the bus, potato, rotten potato who cares!"

Van Go speaks up very loudly, "Don't leave yet, there's more. Bob gave me some files for you to have. Seems like you weren't the only Wall Street guy in the tunnel!"

"You know?"

"Bob was a junk-bond guy way back when he got hooked on the blow and fried his brains. You were the only one to give a rat's ass! You were his hero on his sober days, when he went to the library and got online."

Van Go pauses for a moment and pulls out a rolled-up pile of papers from his man bag.

"Here you go. Hundreds of pages of data, research, your bio, your rise, and fall, everything!"

"Everything!?"

"But wait there's more for you Billy be amazed, account numbers, and names of people, your company screwed over!"

"All the people?"

"But wait, there's even more, Allah sham wow, every digit misplaced and accounted for, plus interest in the Cayman Island, plus the Swiss. Can't Bob's info help with all the damage you signed for as Wadsworth stooge?"

"But wait, there's a mole, Larry, and or curly? Do we cheat them, and how?"

"Maybe Schamp, he was the biggest stooge and never got his due!"

"Wow, now what?"

"To the safe place, bring all the files, we have homework to do!"

Overwhelmingly they then pause and look at Bob's face on the wall. Simultaneously, they chant.

"All for one, and one for all!"

"Van Go, where is Win Thorpe, Coleman, Valentine, and Ophelia, when you need them?"

"That was a movie, I don't think the A Team can help either."

"Coffee and stale doughnuts? I will stop by the bake shop, they throw out the donuts at four, the best dumpster donuts in the big city. Best be at the back door, no sense being a jack in the dumpster, that just scares the bakers."

Quincy takes the lead as they traverse out of the old subway tunnels.

"Okay, let's set our imaginary watches, see you in the a.m., get some rest. This is going to take some time. We've got a put together all the pieces of the puzzle. Long hours, days, nights in between my collections, and my regular duty. Not the kind you find in the pool while the caddies are swimming."

"I agree. Q code word, nutty doughnut!"

"Why am I hungry for a baby Ruth?"

They turn and salute each other and disappear into opposite directions.

Later that day, night has fallen. Todd, the waiter is carrying a large bag like Santa as he comes into the center of the homeless gangs.

"Honey, I'm home! What's for dinner?"

A homeless lady cries out. "There is no dinner!"

Todd replies. "There is now!"

He goes over to make a table upright and unfolds his large ditty bag, boxes and boxes of takeout food. The gang gathers around as he starts to pass out the takeout boxes. Sally, his girlfriend, is the last in line.

"How did you?"

"There was an order for takeout and the guy never showed up. He was some kind of security in the area. He must have been in a hurry. I was lucky to get this off his credit card number before he hung up. Sounded like he was in heavy traffic on the go."

Sally then whispers into Todd's ear.

"You didn't, not that thugs card, tell me you didn't!"

"I did not, but someone else did, the order was called in for dinner and paid for by a credit card, of which an account was set up for future take outs, that's all I know."

Without even saying his name three times, Quincy shows up out of the shadows, followed by the artist.

"What's all this? My trained artistic eye tells me it looks like a Good Samaritan, has donated to the cause."

Quincy looks at it.

"Next time, I hope the delivery doesn't take three hours. I know it's great food, but I wouldn't wait more than an hour and a half." "Even if Wolfgang himself were rattling the pots and pans."

Van Go replies, "Whom did get rattled for all of this?"

Todd jumps back in. "Thunderbolt Incorporated." Some kind of company charge account. They had dined in before. Large groups of men, all in black uniforms."

Quincy, Todd, and Van Go formally known as the artist start to make plans.

"Maybe next time they should actually get what they ordered with the company credit card from behind the street sweeper. Maybe another ride behind the street sweeper might shake loose other things and we can see what else falls out."

"I'll keep an eye out at the food Emporium's. They have many outposts in the city."

"Todd, they might have some lunches delivered tomorrow. I do believe they are stationed at the new high-rise next to the cathedral where I work. Mostly the first floor and the construction area. Maybe with some really hot spices, hey Van Go? Light them up! A number five with jalapenos is pretty tasty."

"If your next to a Mexican fireman!"

The old homeless woman appears out of nowhere, and they are all wide-eyed to see her.

"Young man, thanks for the food. Dumpster diving is a young person's game. Maybe I bring my friends for the next buffet."

"You have me at a loss, Madam, I am the artist formally known as Van Go, this is my friend Padre."

She looks up at Quincy and raises one eyebrow and gives him the once over.

"I already know you. Are you off those IV drugs you were hooked on?"

"Hooked on?" "I haven't been since you took it from me!"

"So, you have been straight all this time?"

"Straight? Yes, thanks for the intervention! I'm better now!" Van Go shakes his head.

"Padre you know her?"

Quincy whispers into Van Go's good ear,

"Yeah, she must be close to 150 years old."

"How does she do it?"

"I may be crazy, but I'm not stupid, and my hearing is above normal. Just because you grow old, it doesn't mean you have to deteriorate!"

Todd is dumbfounded.

"By no means did we imply age, age is a number. Why I've served wine that is at its best when it's almost 50 years old."

The old woman leans forward and bats her eyes at Todd. Then snickering like an old witch, she says.

"I got your number, sweetie! I'm the original hellcat from the cope at studio 54, and the Playboy club. Her name was Lola, she was a showgirl! That was me, the Mandy Pandy, low down, good for nothing. Barry Manilow stole my life story! Tony, Rico, and the Copa, it all happened! The whole town has gone to hell in a shopping cart, I tell you! But you stir my loins. Todd."

Todd backs away little, just as the old woman puckers up, and leans in for a kiss. They all just stand around motionless, then Quincy and the artist look at each other.

"Well, that was different, different strokes for different folks. Todd! She wanted to paint the town with you."

"It takes all kinds, unlike a fine wine. I'd never serve her on the wine list."

The artist turns to Quincy and salutes him.

"So, what do we know about Bob's data and notes?"

Quincy returns a salute,

"Some of it is coherent, about the loss of his job and the people on his shit lists, repeated over and over, and over again. Then bits and pieces of reality pop through. It's gonna, take some time to make anything out of all of it. He named names, he had all the dirt on all the Wall Street, CEOs, workers, and even the cab drivers. He knew. Also, a long list of clients, good and bad, or partly the ones that got screwed by my old boss! There's definitely a connection between Bob's files and a reckoning. Only time will tell. Mr. Mann. Did you see the feather still in Lola's hair?

"Yeah, she looked a little like Barry."

"No, I, you could be right, where was the Copacabana?"

"Not far from here. I will take you there sometime. I did some paintings there. The upstairs is gone, but the subterranean tunnels are still there. They may even have hidden treasures, where the mobsters hung out!"

Moments later, the group of homeless people are finishing their food and cleaning up after themselves. There is a clear area on the dry floor space and Sally comes forth as to announce something.

"Those of you that know me, know that I used to teach dance, or I did until I lost my lease and so forth."

"Sweetheart are you sure your broken ankle is healed enough?"

"Todd, my love, there is no time like the present. Okay everyone that wants to participate, a little bit closer. We'll start with the basics!"

Sally starts to move like a dancer, stretching and bending and flexing.

"Weight shift from right to left, keeping balance is a part of dancing, movement of the arm swaying back and forth with ease, try to feel the music as it moves you. Finding the beat that move your feet, finding a song that moves you along, we get some pep into our step, and some style with a big smile! Like you know a secret. And your body wants to shake, 'cause you just can't keep it inside!"

She continues to dance in place, Todd turns on the boombox with the song sway. The group starts to respond. Although homeless, of all shapes and sizes are doing their own thing, in and out of time to the music. Todd starts to sway with Sally, the group breaks off in pairs. The artist and Quincy are left standing by the side. They look at each other. In another celebrity type voice,

"Marlon Brando, if you will?" Quincy says.

"Not if you were the last tango in Paris!"

"I am a waltz man myself, may be a polka now and then. The Hokey Pokey, or the chicken dance, thank the Lord disco is dead, but I did like the Bee Gees, oh, oh, oh, oh, staying alive! And definitely, no pole dancing! Unless it's with Mrs. Calabash or lonely firemen."

The whole gang seems to be having the time of their lives. They literally dance the night away.

The next day. In the brightness of the sun, the center of attention, is the shiny new bank building. Very tall and mostly glass. Gathering around at the street level are large groups of dignitaries and media people attending a ribbon cutting ceremony. The much older, distinguished looking Wadsworth is standing next to Tim, along with some of the security goons from the encounters with Quincy. The bustling crowd quiets down as Wadsworth speaks into the microphones at the podium. Tim leans in and announces his boss,

"Ladies and Gentlemen, I give you, Mr. Rico Wadsworth!"

The crowd gives a brief applause then Rico speaks,

"I'd like to welcome all of you here today on this special occasion. This building will be my legacy. My many years of hard work have paid off. If there is one thing I have learned, it's that you have to do things for yourself, if you want to get things done right!"

Abruptly, they are interrupted by the large ringing cathedral bells. They ring uncontrollably, drowning out the ribbon-cutting ceremony. Then from out of the sky, falls a large loose church stone. It crashes with a loud boom near the crowd. The dust settles, and they see the church stone, smashed on one of the construction trucks next to the new building. As the crowd looks away from Wadsworth, he tries to divert their attention.

"May I have your attention, attention, that's just the old cathedral, taking its last breath, making room for progress as the new era begins with the beautiful Wadsworth building! We have progressively annexed the nearby lots, as we see deterioration is merely a slow self-demolition. Looking into the future. We dedicate this building to all the clients that believe in our company. We have grown by leaps and bounds!"

Just then a reporter interrupts Wadsworth speech.

"The public wants to know what happened with the 50 clients that you squandered their fortunes with no accountability?"

"What?"

Rico pauses for a moment.

"That was a malicious miss fortune of one man whom took all those people by his lonesome, on his own. My good company, the name of Wadsworth, was cleared of all charges! Now can we get on with the celebration!? The first five floors are complete, the rest of the floors will be homes to complementary companies."

He then takes the big scissors and cuts the big bright red ribbon.

"Let the doors open and all are welcome!"

While the people gather, they began to crowd Wadsworth and his guards as they go through the front door. As the last person pushes through the artist squeezes out back onto the sidewalk. He has a smile on his face, he stops and opens his hand revealing a palm pilot with the initials of R.W. on it, in gold. He shines it, like a mirror, reflecting light up into the bell tower of the cathedral.

"Houston, we have ignition!"

There is a shadowy figure leaning over an opening of the bell tower. Next to his feet. There is a pry bar and a missing block shaped stone. The reflecting light from below illuminates Quincy's face in the shadows.

"The bigger they are, the more they'll crap their pants!"

Quincy leans outward as the wind blows at his figure like Superman's flying cape. He is keeping vigil at his post till the sun begins to set. Then the shadows of nightfall exuding darkness. In the back alley where Quincy keeps his large pushcart, a few of the security goons are nosing around with a flashlight. Then, from inside the cart, pops up, Van Go. He jumps out and starts to run away from the goons. A goon turns and shoots him with a taser gun. It knocks Van Go down, he shakes into unconsciousness. The goons rush to him and start to search him.

"I'm sure this is the guy that stole the bosses' wallet and palm pilot!"

"Best look in the cart again."

One of the other goons looks back inside the cart with his flashlight.

"Nothing!"

The biggest goon goes over to the cart, takes out a cigarette lighter, rolls up some newspaper, and sets fire to the huge pushcart. Van Go lays motionless, and a car goes up in flames behind him. Another goon notices something in the artist's hand.

"Hey, look, it's in his hand!"

Just then emergency sirens are heard off in the distance.

"Got it, let's get out of here!"

The big one agrees, "let's see them make their collections without their favorite pushcart."

"Ya, they are out of the biz."

The dark uniform security goons walk away, cocky, into the dark, talking to one another.

"Hey, did you order flam Bay Ala cart?"

"Ain't the Big Apple, great! If were down south, we would have had to wear white sheets!" The artist is still curled up on the ground as Quincy shows up and hovers over him. He helps him to his feet.

"Are you okay?"

"I'm alive, but your cart!"

The cart is in flames behind them.

"It's the toast of the town! The other collectors will be so jealous. They got the palm pilot. Van Go!"

Van Go replies. "That was close but no cigar."

He opens his hand and shows Quincy, the Sim card.

"You got the Sim card on the palm pilot."

"Everything you could possibly want to know about Rico Wadsworth is on this card. Q."

"How so pothole water breath? Geez, you need to be hosed down. You smell like a crockpot gone wrong!"

"Yeah, 1000 volts will steam cook your marbles!"

"As long as you don't lose them, I got to get you settled in and hit the collections they are all behind."

"How?"

"Not to worry my little fried friend."

The night is still new as Quincy goes walking down the city streets. The streetlights are half burned out, but still shine on things somewhat. He takes shortcuts and does what he does to complete his goals. Then, from out of the darkness, 30 shopping carts linked together filled with cans. There is an automatic shopping cart mover with a yellow blinking light being pushed by Quincy. He is laboring as the carts try to snake away from him. He starts to sing as he makes his way down the street,

"16 carts, what do you get, another day older and deeper in debt, St. Peter don't you call me because I can't go, I owe my soul to the homeless, I know! Oh yeah, oh yeah, oh yeah."

Still in mission mode, he makes it back to meet Van Go. He takes care of all his recyclables. Quincy and Van Go head to the library roof. They find an entrance point and sneak in like cat burglars through the skylight. Once inside, Quincy is led by Van Go to the computer room in the back of a library. They move quickly into the room and shut the door behind them. There is only one computer on. The screen illuminates Quincy and the artists face as they sit side-by-side. Quincy clicks on a keyboard.

"Hand me that sim card to put into the external device."

"Q, you got that plugged in, right?"

"Yep, should just about be ready to open the files, and there it is! Look at that private offshore accounts. Between this analysts Bob made, we should be able to write, some wrongs."

Quincy pauses for a second as his condition dictates.

"It's still like paint by numbers man. Yet, two wrongs don't make a right. But if you are up on the top two wrongs you might fall. Wadsworth's ladder of success is going to be pretty wobbly in the near future!"

Quincy is still tapping away at the keyboard as fast as he can.

"You gonna crack this code, or what?"

"No Maas da Vinci, you said code." "This will take some time, might as well break out the dumpster doughnuts and the coffee thermos." "These library computers aren't the fastest."

Van Go looks over Quincy shoulder at the computer screen.

"What's that?"

"Pop-ups."

"What's E.D? It says I need help?"

"You don't want to know, just click the "X" and it will disappear."

"Another one, this one's about lonely animals."

Quincy goes off on another side thought as he clears the pop-ups.

"Old Mick Wadsworth had a farm, eiei he's gotta to go!"

"You like music, don't you Q?"

"Back in the day I had quite the eight-track tape selection. You'd spend all your money on those bulky things. You didn't know if the tape broke until it unraveled inside the player. Then after the music stopped, you had a broken eight-track tape. The only reason I had such a large collection, is because I made money from the Lear Corporation in stocks. You see, they were the cutting edge in technology. The same guy made the Lear Jets."

"Are you telling me that the eight-track was invented by Lear who invented the Lear Jet's?"

"One and the same, oh look, another pop-up." "Do you need Viagra and Rogaine?" "Be a new man buy the combo package, but don't misuse you might end up with stiff hair and a curly wang!"

"Yeah, don't mix them up, the side effects alone might end up in all your problems."

"Look a money back guarantee!"

"Really?"

"But wait there's more, if you can't comb, you'll be alone, it'll make pointers out of setters, it made Richard switch gears, Brad a pit, Conan a barbarian, Robert Stack, Zig "free" Roy, gave Bob Hope, made Lucille Ball, Isaac Hayes, Jimmy Dean, Howard Stern, Jack Black, Tom Cruise, Jerry Stiller, Iggy Pop, A Rod, and even LeeAnn Rimes."

"You said a mouthful."

"That to if you play for the other team. You're not a switch hitter, are you?"

"I already told you I wouldn't dance with you, pass that box of dumpster doughnuts over here.

"Who ate, all the cream sticks?"

"Get over it, I always got table scraps when I was home. Being the smallest in the family. You had to learn to be quick when food was on the table. Why do you think I let you do all the typing? A ploy? Just to eat the good doughnuts?! I left the bear claws for you."

"There is no creamy center in those, and some of the others were custard filled. That may not be the last straw, but it was the last stand."

"Q, Custer died at the last stand. Have some respect!"

"A good hot falafel, would be good right now!"

"Beggars can't be choosy, Q."

"At least there are more falafel carts, then you and your appetite can keep up with."

"It's more greed than hunger, I think I got a bellyache."

"Just how many of those did you eat big pig?"

"I lost track, we have been here for hours."

"You have been sneaking, all this time. While I have been doing the work."

"While you been doing all the talkin', it was easy."

"Starving artist. My semi-sculptured half ass."

"Don't try to change the subject with humor."

"You cream stick, long John, the pirate! I think you do have issues, I'm sleeping with my back to the gutter tonight."

"Q come on, get your mind out of the gutter, focus, we have to complete operation, nutty doughnut."

"All ones with nuts are gone to, speaking of music, who's your favorite artist?"

"Bette Midler."

"I knew it! Nothing but show tunes and Bette Midler, on your eight track tapes. That's the 6 degrees of separation, Barry Manilow used to play it for Bette, the old woman was the Copa girl in the song. Music and romance at the Coppola, Copacabana. The jury ain't out no more, I rest my case, oh look another pop-up, are you lonely, meet new exciting young men online, is that a, picture of you? My bad, it's a young man's site. They say they can ring your bell."

"Just because I said Bette Midler, doesn't mean I am that way, I am an artist, I painted her nude when she was just starting out. She was a starving artist as well, we ate out a lot back in those days, we had hot dog vendors everywhere, I think she really cared about me."

"You were doing good till the wiener and the bun affixation, they were everywhere! The next time you see Betty, just ask her who's gay? I'm thinking most of her fans."

"Just one minute, hold your horses, stop the presses, you're the one obsessed singing about the missing cream sticks there Sigmund Freud, thou dost protest too much. Okay, so they're just doughnuts, and the bag of doughnut holes. There are a few chocolate balls left, isn't there?"

"Really... those too?"

"We still got coffee?"

"Lots."

"I'm good and needed to wash down the stale bear claws, don't let me choke."

"No problem, I know the high lick maneuver!"

Quincy doesn't say a word, but gives him a funny look and just shakes his head no.

"Q, this is getting us nowhere fast."

"Besides Van, we just hit a brick wall, we need a password, without the password it won't let as do anything."

"Wadsworth's personal password, oh, that could be anything damn!"

The boys call it quits. They disperse from the scene until the big event.

Now in a new time and place. In the City Civic Center, is the Halloween charity event. There are many people in various costumes arriving in limos. The crowd meanders between the marble columns with a "Children's Fund" sign overhead, arriving inside. The atrium is decorated with fancy Halloween trimmings. There are sidebars at a large buffet area, people are serving themselves. Fruits, vegetables, breads, desserts, a chef is cutting and serving the people prime rib, as well as lobster, and crab cakes. There is a live band playing dinner music, quiet, subdued in the background. Some people are on the dance floor, others standing in small groups, drinking, talking, and others are seated eating buffet. There is a small group talking and in the center of the group is Rico Wadsworth. Rico in all his splendor and glory, is dressed as George Washington. Standing next to him by his side is his niece Fanny dressed as snow white.

"This is a fabulous party Fanny, each year you outdo yourself." "I understand there will be special entertainment?"

"You are too kind, but it's all just part of my function to take from the rich and give it to the poor, and the unfortunate."

"You are the rich, my dear!"

"Rich but not powerful like you, uncle, with money I have obligations to consider." "I'm not in the game like you are uncle." "Are you still playing winner takes all?"

"Not so much as I mature, but I do guard my winnings." "Charity begins at home, if you give everything you have a way. There is no security." "You have to have a buffer zone to protect against the unforeseeable."

"Unforeseeable is that when you keep a blind eye to the social plights of your fellow man is that it uncle?"

"Willingness to work hard, has kept my status, and I will continue to do so. I'm here for your charity events. Isn't that enough said!"

"Yes, thank you uncle that is true and the donations have always been more than adequate."

"I merely pass the buck to all my employees, it's a team effort, we must all do our fair share after all. Speaking of that, I think that man in that disheveled grumpy costume, the lobster lover, that is his third plate since we have been talking. The matter of fact is, the whole group behind him in line may as well have pulled up chairs. Tim go check that out!"

"No, it's my party. I am responsible."

Tim, Wadsworth's number one stooge, follows Fanny anyways. She goes up to grumpy and taps him on the back.

"Excuse me, Mr. grumpy, are you and your friends enjoying yourself sufficiently?"

Quincy dressed as grumpy turns to acknowledge her. He has on the Disney adult grumpy costume, a large hat covering half of his face to one side, a large oversize nose, as well as a large stuffed bodysuit, making him look very animated. Quincy is caught off guard as he just took a bite of gourmet cupcake. The thick frosting, is all over his lips and it inhibits his response. He almost responds by calling out her name, but he catches himself.

"Fan." He pauses. "Fantastic! Ma'am, great! The frosted cake is great, thank you for asking."

Then Tim interrupts.

"May we see your invitation sir?"

Then suddenly from behind Quincy, Sally appears dressed as a scary cat. She leans forward and interrupts Tim.

"I have all the invites, we came as a group, a dance troupe."

Looking at them all, Sally extends her hand and waves with approval.

"I hope so they look like living dead bums, oh my Lord, what smells like somebody crapped a pine tree?"

"Sir, I am Sally Rivers, of the Sally Rivers Dance Academy." "We are this evenings special entertainment."

Quincy laughingly interjects.

"Yes, special, definitely special!"

Then Fanny leans forward looking Quincy in the eye. Quincy quickly turns to Sally and grabs her arm.

"It's Showtime Sally, let's not keep the good folks waiting."

He pulls her over, by the arm, to the bandleader, to talk with him for a few. Then Sally takes the mic, as if to make an announcement. She stops and strangely leads all her friends through some fake cobwebs in the nearby doorway. The group, in their everyday wear, covered in cobwebs look very entertaining. Sally goes back to the mic.

"Ladies and gentlemen for your entertainment from the Sally Rivers Dance Academy, the Sally Rivers Dance Troupe."

The lights go low, and the music-based beat starts up beginning slow and sure.

Quincy grabs Sally around the arm and pulls her close to him and whispers.

"Now what?"

"You have missed practice, just stay in the last line and try to keep up."

The homeless dance troupe, looking very disheveled begin. The band plays the song, Thriller. The troop reacts properly doing the whole dance. The scary strobe lights and the fog machine cover the whole area. Quincy is in the back line near the exit. Fanny standing near Rico starts to think. Her expressions on her face are blank. She's troubled yet thinking about something.

"Great Frosted Cakes, Face! No, that can't be true, that's impossible! Quincy?"

The music stops, the lights go up, and the dancers disappear. No grumpy, no nothing. Fanny looks around and grabs one of the dancer's arms. It's Lola, the old woman covered with cobwebs.

"Please can you help me? Maybe you can be of service to me."

"Sure. But, first, who's that handsome looking George Washington?"

"That's my uncle, Rico Wadsworth."

The old woman stops and stares blankly. Then, Fanny shakes her a little, and she pulls away.

"Don't leave, who was that man dressed in the grumpy costume? Please tell me, tell me please don't leave."

The old woman laughs, she cackles, then she makes an evil face.

"Don't ask for whom the bells toll, the bells, the bells. They never stop ringing." Then she scurries away.

Meanwhile, on the front steps, Quincy has stopped to rest for a moment. A costumed group of people get out of the limo directly in front of him. Yes, it is the village people. They walk towards Quincy as they go into the building. The one guy dressed as a cop asked concerned,

"Hey grumpy, come back inside. You know we'll be dancing in five minutes, maybe six. Maybe we can cheer you up, besides, isn't that snow white up there looking for you at the top of the steps!?"

Quincy looks over his shoulder and sees Fanny searching around. He pushes quickly past the village people and jumps into the open door of their limo.

"Driver quickly back to the hotel we forgot the sailor!"

The limo squeals its tires and leaves just as Fanny gets to the bottom of the stairs. She looks down and around, and then picks up something from where grumpy was sitting. A bell-shaped soap on a rope.

"Pine!"

Fanny is perplexed, as the evening expires.

A very short time later.... There is a light on in the corner of the library computer room. It hangs over a round table with people setting around it. Quincy and friends are playing cards. Quincy is in rare form, as he wears a dealer's sun visor tilted to one side.

"I'll bet two."

Going around the table. The artist's is next.

"I'll see your two and I'll bet you three, Q."

"I didn't make enough tips tonight, I fold! You guys are too rich for my little pair of deuces."

"I dropped a pair of deuces earlier."

Sam, the retired librarian, is next to the waiter, it's his turn.

"Talk, talk, talk, that's all you ladies do. If you want to play with women, then go play with women. That would spell trouble though. If you don't believe me, just look at the word. WOMAN, take away the W and what do you have, OMEN and that spells trouble. It's a man's game, I'll see, your four and raise you two."

"That's two to you, Padre."

"What up or shut up, that is pretty ballsy for an old lady that folds."

"I'm not so old."

"Don't ever break the law son because you would bawl like an old lady in the pen."

"Sam, have you been there?"

Van Go snorts and laughs.

"No, but I just watched it, Shawshank, and it ain't pretty."

Todd raises an eyebrow.

"How is it we get to hang out here after-hours Sam? You are the librarian, ain't you breaking the law?"

"The gambler's anonymous meeting." "I posted on the bulletin board in the library."

Van Go nods at Sam.

"Yeah, he's too proud, he's one of us, since they cut his hours. Sam, here is a part timer after 20 years. To cut his expenses, he dwells here after hours at this fine establishment just like me. If they released him, it wouldn't be good, no home."

Todd shrugs his shoulders.

"I've never heard of a bad release, except for that first old guy in Shawshank."

"Yeah, he hung in there till the very end."

"Yes, I got family, all grown up. After my wife died, cut backs and all, I wouldn't think of moving in with my grown kids. I still have enough to visit them on holidays and I still got some healthcare. By sleeping here. I am always on time for work. Now, can we stop with the jawing and play poker? "

Quincy is drinking a beer and chugs it all down. Sam nudges him,

"Padre are you in, that's two to you?"

Without skipping a beat. Quincy smashes one beer can on the top of his head, then another, takes the flat cans and tosses them on top of the pile of flat cans in the center of the poker game.

"Call!"

Quincy burps, then farts. Sam holds his nose and fans the air with his free hand.

"Man smells like a drunk skunk that shit out some pine cones." Sam tosses down his cards face up.

"Three of a kind."

Mr. fine arts contributes.

"Two pair, it's up to you stinky."

Before Quincy lays down his cards, he perks up, then pauses like he lost his train of thought. (Another side effect of his extensive injuries.) He holds onto his gold cross around his neck.

"Being a man of the cloth. I sometimes wonder about things in life. Have you gentlemen ever heard of the Immusketlet Conception?"

They all respond strangely with question in their voice. Sam librarian, a little louder than the others.

"You mean the Immaculate Conception?"

"No musket, it was during the Civil War. Before Johnny came marching home. He got shot right through the scrotum! It proceeded to go through the window of Miss Scarlett's plantation house. Yet imbedded into her woman parts slightly enough as to cause an injury, but after she was bandaged up. Nine months later. Immusketlet Conception!"

Van Go is in disbelief.

"Can you believe this crap Sam, you really can shovel it."

"I think it's a true story."

Then Quincy lays down a royal flush.

"Roy Al flush!"

"That figures Q."

"What's that?" Sam replies.

"A royal flush, he craps then he flushes."

Todd puts his hands over his nose and mouth.

"That stinks, no really, someone opened a freakin' window."

They all make faces. Quincy is bobbing up and down like he's had way too much to drink.

"Padre, are you okay?"

"Yeah, just shut up and deal!"

"What a grumpy winner!"

Quincy lashes out uncontrollably.

"Grumpy, snow white, dammit all!"

Sam reaches out to Q.

"Sorry man, you want to talk about it?"

Then the others follow,

"No, leave him alone, he's been drinking."

"Should we take a break?"

Quincy chimes in, "No, we play to forget, let's keep going. That's the last beer anyways."

"What?" "Why did you, take the last one!"

"Like you took all the dumpster doughnuts, starving artist my ass!"

Quincy starts to slur, just little bit. He speaks,

"My name is Quincy M. Otto!"

Then he passes out on the poker table.

Todd the waiter is laughing a little.

"He said Quasimodo!"

Sam joins in,

"Quincy M. Otto." "That's the hunchback of Wall Street! That ain't right, but it's funny."

Van Go shakes his head no.

"Stop, it's not funny, but the truth is sometimes funnier than fiction. He rings the bells at the Cathedral. His face is a person only a mother could love. What happened in the library stays in the library."

Then all the sudden Quincy perks up seeming completely sober. (A strange phenomenon of his abnormal human condition of survival.)

"My mom loved me, my fanny loved me, I loved me, but no matter how the kids used to make fun of my name, I was proud just the same. That's it, that's it! The glorious bastard!"

Quincy stands up and looks at the artist.

"To the bat computer Robin!"

Then they get up and go over to the one computer that is still on in the corner of library. They all join in and are sitting around the computer as it illuminates their faces. This time you see Quincy's entire deformed face as he is a living Picasso painting. He works the computer keyboard feverishly almost building up a sweat.

"That's it we're in! "Quincy M. Otto", it was the password! That bastard thought he buried his pass, now it's back to bite him in the financial ass. Elvis has left the building, good night, Mrs. Calabash wherever you are, that's the way it was, frankly, my dear, I don't give a damn, put the lotion in the basket, the humanities, the horror, the whore, I'm too old for this, Bueller, Bueller! Yo, Fanny. We did it!"

Then he passes out, slumped over the table. Van Go covers him with a blanket. Then the lights are turned off, so one man may drift off into dreams, hopefully calling an end to some of his suffering.

The smell of morning coffee freshly brewed is in the air. A large mug with the word "BOSS" monogrammed on it, is carefully placed on a large executive desk by Tim, the executive assistant. Hot coffee steams and vapors throughout the room, like fog. Rico was in his large, high back leather chair, looking out the window of his office building. In his view, he contemplates the old cathedral, and its Gothic allure. His back is to Tim and the coffee. Rico starts to swivel his big chair around and bellows,

"Tim, Tim, get in here!"

Rico was a little startled as his coffee is already in front of him and Tim is standing at attention waiting for orders.

"Yes sir, how may I be of assistance to you today?"

"Tim, what's the progress of the annexation of the old cathedral?"

"I'm on it, sir."

"You'd better be, your retirement account matures this quarter. With all the years of service that should be a tidy sum. Hey Tim? Have you checked the status on those accounts recently?"

"No, sir, I have been very busy with the annexation."

"And?"

"The annexation can only happen if the homeless station, that the Monsignor set up, fails. Fail means, if no one continues to seek aid there and the charitable funds are cut off. It seems the man in charge takes it to the street. He's barely keeping it functioning, by collecting cans and taking donations and so forth. But wait, there is more. Your own company donated last year paying the energy bill, utilities, the electric, and the water."

"Enough is enough. Tim, it's bad enough that the squatters are hanging out in the tunnels under the site project area. How can I reopen the subway stations with two legged rats ruining everything? The whole development is at risk, you go and push this project through."

"I'll check on the status of the special accounts."

Tim leaves the room like a soldier turning on his heels. Rico turns to a large green computer terminal and starts to type on the keyboard with loud sharp taps.

"Damn this thing to hell. The password isn't working, crap I forgot the M. There we go, and the winner is?"

The computer starts to go nuts. The screen flashes in front of Rico's face. It illuminates his stress and anger as he is becoming frustrated.

"Tim, Tim, get in here what's going on with this gadget?"

Tim comes rushing in from the side door. He looks at the screen and starts to type next to Rico.

"It's a malfunction, let's try enter and delete, we'll reboot, that should do it."

He continues tapping on the keys and then he sees the screen. "Cayman Island Bank." There are many accounts on a list, up and down the screen.

"Here is the total of our accounts as to date as they are."

Tim turns white and then shouts.

"Frozen, frozen, frozen!"

Rico is now in full panic.

"Frozen my big, butt! Fix that!"

"It's sending me to customer service, I'll push enter."

The computer voice emits out over the speaker.

"The selection you have made is a frozen account, as of yesterday's transaction at the request of the password holder."

"Is that some kind of trick, to cheat me out of my years of servitude, Rico!"

"I would never."

"If you didn't and I didn't, then who? How?

"Hit that security selection of my toolbar Tim, it has a tracking device for all my transactions. Click on it!"

"It's a list, of the "Offshore Funds of Wadsworth". To be transferred, upon a new password being installed in the transaction."

"Who initiated that transaction, Tim?"

"You're not going to believe this!
Account Manager: Quincy M. Otto.

"What? No, that was the password? Quincy is dead. That's impossible! I saw his corpse at the hospital after the explosion. Trace the computer, whoever access the accounts, and you'll find the cock sucker behind all of this, I'm ruined, I lost everything!"

Rico turns and grabs Tim by the collar. As he stands up from his chair.

"Fix it, dammit, fix it. Damn you, you said he was dead!"

Tim breaks loose from the choke hold, Rico has on his neck.

"Get your damn hands off me, you damn filthy old man! I'm the only friend you have left! I was hoping that the booze or the workers would kill you and send you to an early grave. You even got a liver transplant, just so you could continue drinking. If it wasn't for me, those people that died in the subway, and their donor cards I forged for you, you'd been done a long time ago. We harvest vital organs from semi-healthy, homeless people, you bastard!"

"You did that for me?"

"I had to, you entrusted me with the secret password to the offshore accounts. Damn you."

Tim turns and grabs Rico by the collar then backs off as Rico pushes him away. Tim looked shocked, as there is a pearl handled, gold, 38 Saturday night special, pistol pointed straight into Tim's belly. Just one of many of Rico's engraved guns with his initials on it.

"So that's how it is? It's my game and the fat lady ain't singing yet, so get this shit straightened out. Go find that bastard. Have the boys drop a little surprise down the old tunnels. Get all the closed subway accesses under our feet. If we rid ourselves of the small rodents, the big rat should show his face. Now go set the trap, release the hounds! Release the hounds!"

Wadsworth laughs uncontrollably like a crazy mad scientist.

Soon thereafter in the abandoned sub way tunnels... Dimly lit as usual, the sun coming through the drain and manholes of the streets above, a few of the underground homeless are moving around. Possibly about 50 or so, living, breathing, and sleeping. Through the vents, smoke starts to creep and cloud in from all areas. The sleeping homeless slowly get covered in the foggy mist. Down one of the side tunnels, the artist is painting on the walls. He sees the cloud of gas creeping towards him. He reacts quickly, climbing to the surface, and opens a manhole cover to let in some air and the smoke out. Van Go climbs out coughing as the cloud follows him. He sees a large tank truck and some of the security guards with a hose going into the street vents, into the ground, sending the gas down under. Van Go crawls up on his feet coughing as he goes over to the truck. He takes a pry bar and starts down the middle of the street, opening as many manhole covers as he can. One of the goons sees him

"Hey, that artist guy is nuts, grab 'em. He's the rat bastard that picked the bosses' pockets!"

Three of the security guards dressed in black chase him down. They drag him back to the tanker truck. The tallest one speaks,

"Pack it up, the cops will be here soon. Let's roll."

Not too far away at the hospitals overflowing ICU ward. The place is overflowing with patients filling all the rooms. Familiar faces of the homeless. The nurses and the doctors are all busy, then one of the alarms goes off over the PA system.

"Code blue, number 15, code blue!"

The doors to the ICU unit fly open as Quincy, in his hooded robe enters and goes over Todd in one of the rooms. He is by Todd's side. Todd is on oxygen. Quincy holds his hand. Todd opens his eyes and tries to sit up. Quincy holds him down.

"Easy kid. What happened, I was out on the collections run when I went to make my rounds with the group. The whole 911 squad was picking up my people!"

"I was heading back to Sally after work. Down the secret elevator. She was already passed out from the smoke at the bottom. I dragged her backup topside and I called 911, while I was on the phone I saw artist being taken away by those thugs with the thunderbolt patches. They were in a gas tanker type truck, the big hose from the tanker was dragging behind them. It bounced, and I got hit. They, they got Van Go man, they got him, I need to." Todd passes out.

"Rico!"

Quincy turns and starts to walk to the nearest elevator and a nurse stops him. He has his back to her.

"Father, thank you for coming, we lost two of them earlier, the older ones, the others will be some time."

Quincy turns and puts a hand on the nurses' eyes covering them.

"Bless you."

Then he steps fast into the open elevator and it closes.

Nearby is the old cathedral, a local landmark, in all its Gothic splendor. At the top of the bell tower, there is movement within. Quincy and Sam are up in the bell tower moving things around, large box shape things. They are running cords and gear. They are up to something. But what? Then the moment is revealed, about 100 odd microphones bungee corded together. Walls of black boxes are formed in the openings of the bell tower. Almost all the openings are blocked, up to the roof line. Quincy reaches over to a volume control on the electronic board. A black dial with numbers around it up to the number 10. Quincy speaks.

"What number?"

Sam replies, "11."

Then Quincy and Sam face one another, shake hands, and salute one another. The bell tower is packed to its rafters from the normal openings, now filled with walls and walls of black speaker boxes of various sizes, then we hear the large cathedral bells start to ring. Slowly, then faster and faster until the noise rings loud over the gigantic speaker system. The guys both put their hands over their ears because of the high decibel levels. The bell tower is directly across from the shiny, brand-new, Wadsworth building. The noise emits, and a few large windows start to crack. One by one they all shatter and crash to the ground between the building and the old cathedral. Shortly there after the bells die down and it is revealed that the entire side between the two structures is bare. Windows are all destroyed. The sun sets on all the glittering devastation. Quincy has reached the point of no return. He and his cause, are now fully committed.

Retaliation is swift. The next day in the abandoned subways, the security guards in black are marching in force, about 20 of them. They walk one end to the other, flashing flashlights and guns through the underground village of the homeless. Eventually they find the artist, and start escorting him, pushing him at gunpoint. They stop when they find a fairly lit up spot where the sunlight is beaming through the vents overhead. Just then, from a side tunnel, Quincy appears. He has a large sized envelope in his hands. An uneven standoff. Quincy on one side, the security guards holding the artist on the other. The tall security guard speaks,

"Okay, hand it over, the boss needs the new password."

"The artist walks, then I'll hand it over to you."

"Whatever."

The artist is freed. He gets about 20 feet away and Quincy throws the envelope like a frisbee way past the security squad, over their heads. They scramble to get it.

"Run Van Go."

They all scatter in confusion. The head security guard yells.

"After them, you idiots. The boss wants them alive!"

Van Go yells.

"Down this way. Q, you always wanted to see the Copacabana."

They rush into a dark area. Quincy uses a flashlight to find a small boarded up access tunnel. They pull some of the boards down and go in. Quincy flashes around with his flashlight. They see empty wine bottles, old chairs, and club tables with lots of cobwebs. Van Go takes the flashlight from Quincy,

"Here behind the poster of the Copacabana."

The artist takes down a framed poster of the Copacabana. There is a hole in the wall. He reaches in and pulls out a wad of cash.

"We are running for our lives and you stop for Al Capone's ATM?"

Then the artist pulls out a long rifle type of gun.

"Now what?" Quincy looks puzzled.

"It's a BAR!"

"I know it's a bar, the Copacabana."

Then Van Go pulls out a 20 round clip, snaps it into the rifle and racks it back.

"Browning Automatic Rifle, look at this."

There is also a gold plated 45 caliber pistol with a pearl handle. He hands it over to Quincy. He looks at it very closely. The pistol is engraved in gold on the side. "RICO."

"Our little monster is all grown up, where did we go wrong? What did I say about two wrongs? Junior needs a spanking. His mama didn't hug him enough when he was little. Ready? Let's do this!"

"It's your coming-out party, you lead."

"Again, with the cream stick issues?"

The security guards go right past them in the main tunnel. Quincy steps out into the light from the side tunnel. One of the goons in black spots him.

"There he is."

They all turn and face him. Van Go stays back in the shadows. Then, from the crowd of goons, Rico steps forward, he plants his feet firmly in front of his men. Quincy is standing with his arms down by his side facing the group. The odds are stacked against him. Rico makes a speech.

"You're trapped you big rat, why couldn't you have stayed dead like the good little preppy, that you were."

"I never went to college, you textbook smart ass."

"My niece wanted you, but I didn't. So, you survived all this time, the hunchback of Wall Street! Ha ha ha ha, I'm so scared, but if you want something done right, you have got to do it yourself. Now what's the password to unfreeze all that money you pilfered for me, or the girl gets it!"

Sally is brought forth in front of the security guards dressed in black. She struggles to get free to no avail.

"All right, you win. It's your nieces' name, Fanny. Now let Sally go!"

They let her go, and she walks behind Quincy. One of the big security guards steps forward with a laptop and holds it as Rico types on it. "F-A-N-N-Y."
The computer makes an announcement.

"Access   granted,   all   funds   transferred."
"Transferred!"

Rico looks and smiles.

"All the funds are now transferred into Fanny's personal account, well done, bravo Quincy, but I can deal with her, now say goodbye Quincy."

Quincy extends his hand with the gold 45,

"Hold it, you despicable varmint. If you let us go, no one will get hurt."

"Go ahead punk you feeling ugly, that's my old friend, shoot me if you must, it will probably blow up in your face from corrosion for the last 50 years."

Quincy looks at the gun, then tries to cock the hammer back and it won't move.

"SH I T!"

Rico pulls back his coat, revealing his holster with his gun on his hip, like an old cowboy in an old movie.

"But this one's got a hair trigger, so drop it freak!"

Rico reaches for his gun, then all of a sudden, the artist comes forward, and lets out a burst of semi-automatic rounds. He shoots all above their heads, not to hit anybody. They all dive to the ground, into the sides, and out of the way.

"Run Quincy, run Sally."

Quincy and Sally start to run, and Rico stands back up. Rico's goons are on all sides, still spread out on the ground, taking cover.

"Stop dead in your tracks. Quincy." "He's out of bullets, I only had 12 rounds and that rifle."

"You sure?" Van Go spouts.

Van Go looks at the gun, pulls the clip out, and looks at the empty clip.

"Damn." Van Go Rushes Rico.

Rico shoots him in the leg and he falls to the ground landing on his side.

"I still got it." Ha ha ha ha and now for you Quincy, my Windows?" "Really?" "That was cocky, so no more cock."

Rico aims for Quincy's groin, but shoots him in the middle of his thigh. Quincy goes down and falls beside Van Go. Sally rushes over to help him.

"That was a little sloppy. I should've counted for wind age little more to the left."

Just then the tunnel begins to shake like it's an earthquake. Rico is, unknowingly, standing out in the center of the tracks.

"Now what?" "An earthquake, are you kidding me?"

He's looking perplexed. Rico looks down as his feet. His right foot is now trapped in the tracks. He tries to frantically wiggle his foot out of its confines. Everything continues to shake. They hear a horn blast; the earthquake is coming around the bend. He sees headlights. An old subway workers maintenance engine is barreling down the tracks. Rico starts to yell for help, but nobody's paying attention. He is trapped. Rico's impending doom, is revealed by an old woman that sticks her head out the window of the oncoming train. It's Lola! The old showgirl from the Copacabana. She screams,

"This one is for Tony!" "Die, die, die, you greasy bastard!"

She effortlessly flattens Rico and continues rumbling down the tracks. It's over, everything has gone full circle. What goes around comes around. Karma is a Bitch! Although in this instant, her name was Lola, she was a showgirl, at the Copa, Copacabana! What about the rest? Can there be enough hope or any kind of closure, or is there just the struggle?

Above ground at one of the highest points in the city, Quincy is standing in the opening of the bell tower, a shadowy figure with his hooded cape blowing in the wind. The setting sun is gleaming through making his figure glow in an almost three-dimensional energy. He's near the edge of the ledge. A caped superhero staring out over his city contemplating life. Quincy is startled by a voice somewhere behind him in the bell tower.

"If ever I saw eyes that could see through me and through tomorrow, they would be yours!" "Seriously?" "Snow White and the seven dwarfs, you always knew I loved grumpy best!"

Quincy stays up on the ledge motionless. The wind gives his clothing cape like qualities as they unfurled.

"I, I, I won't, I'm done."

Fanny rushes in from the shadows and reaches for him. He steps to the side and will not let her touch him.

"I can't live anymore like this. There is nothing left of me. I, I can't go on."

"Stop! I know you feel confused, exhausted, and irreconcilably indifferent. As though you have nothing to live for, because of your condition, pain-and-suffering, and grief you've incurred. I know you, you wouldn't jump to save your own life, but you would jump to save mine. Fanny moves closer as she speaks.

"Top of the World Ma!" Quincy yells.

Fanny reacts, quickly grabbing Quincy's leg. Quincy leans further forward towards the edge.
Holding on for dear life, Fanny yells,

"You have a daughter, you have a daughter! She is beautiful and wonderful and has your eyes. Even your lovable sense of humor. We can't and will not live without you!"

He drops to his knees and sobs. Fanny reaches for him, pulling him in, away from the edge. The sun setting illuminates the two of their faces. His good side is showing as she turns to him. Fanny reaches up and removes his hood with both hands. She holds his face in her hands. They stare at each other, partly laughing and partly crying. They hug and kiss in a romantic silhouette. Time stands still, as if they had never been apart.
She whispers to him,

"Even with a frosted face, they're great!"

www.ingramcontent.com/pod-product-compliance
Lightning Source LLC
Chambersburg PA
CBHW061255170626
46809CB00007B/3008